This book is dedicated to my
wonderful grandchildren, Alexis,
Lyndsey, and Rhett. They named the
famous raccoon, Big Daddy!

www.mascotbooks.com

Hurricane on Fripp Island:
A Big Daddy Adventure

For more information, please contact:
Mascot Books
620 Herndon Parkway #320
Herndon, VA 20170
info@mascotbooks.com

Library of Congress Control Number: 2019901279

CPSIA Code: PRT0319A
ISBN-13: 978-1-64307-328-6

Printed in the United States

Hurricane on Fripp Island

A Big Daddy Adventure

Written by Mary T. Jacobs

Illustrated by Alycia Pace

Grandfather was at home watching the news on Fripp Island one day when suddenly, the latest weather report flashed across the TV screen. The news was interrupted for a special report, so Grandfather leaned forward in his chair to make sure he heard every word. He would always remember this October 5th and the evacuation that was to come!

Oh my! thought Grandfather. Governor Haley was addressing the people of South Carolina. She carefully reported that many parts of South Carolina would have to evacuate due to Hurricane Matthew. The governor went on to say, "Residents are advised to leave their homes and go to safer locations."

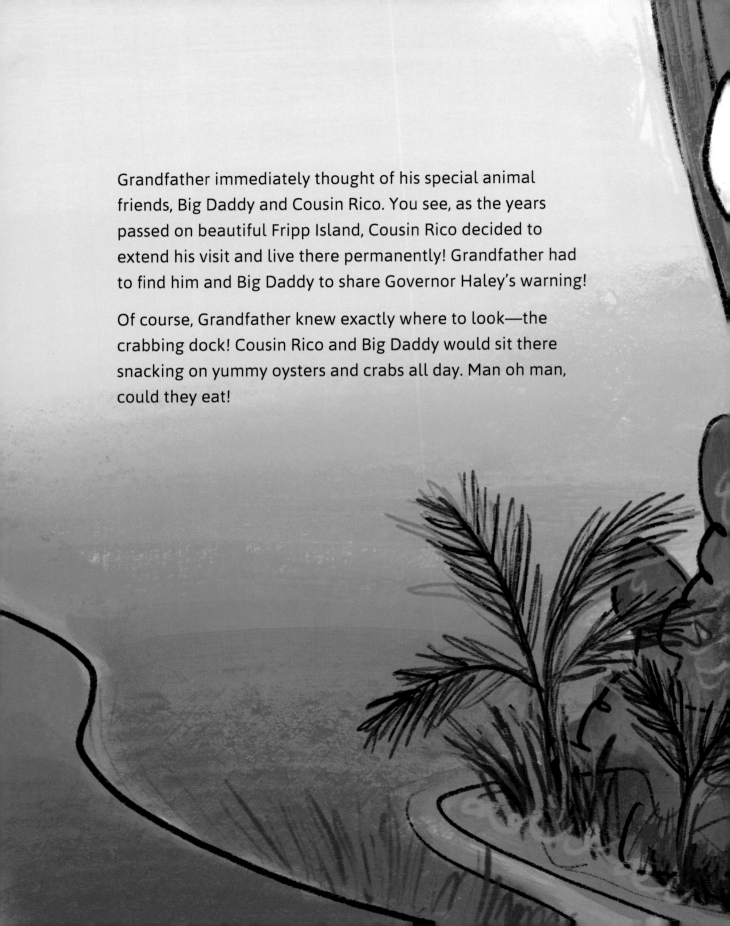

Grandfather immediately thought of his special animal friends, Big Daddy and Cousin Rico. You see, as the years passed on beautiful Fripp Island, Cousin Rico decided to extend his visit and live there permanently! Grandfather had to find him and Big Daddy to share Governor Haley's warning!

Of course, Grandfather knew exactly where to look—the crabbing dock! Cousin Rico and Big Daddy would sit there snacking on yummy oysters and crabs all day. Man oh man, could they eat!

As Grandfather approached, Big Daddy jumped to his feet. "What's wrong?" he asked.

Grandfather told Big Daddy and Cousin Rico about the evacuation and the other things Governor Haley reported.

They reassured Grandfather that they knew what to do in a hurricane, but also recommended that he and Grandmother heed the Governor's warning and leave the island as soon as possible. After all, Governor Haley told all of South Carolina that they must evacuate. If anyone refused to evacuate, rescue personnel would not be able to come for help.

Early the next morning, Grandfather and Grandmother headed south to stay with family on the mainland. As they drove from the island, both were fearful of what could happen, but had faith and confidence that things would be okay. Every day for ten days, Grandfather and Grandmother held hands and prayed for the safety of the animals on the island.

In the meantime, Big Daddy and Cousin Rico rushed around to warn the other animals on the island to take shelter as best as they could.

Hurricane Matthew hit the island the next day and he was strong! The wind was gusting over 100 miles per hour and there were lots of strong storm surges.

All that Fripp families could do was wait and listen to news reports. Only a few folks stayed behind on the island—Big Daddy was not pleased with that decision.

After about ten days, people began returning to the island. They were driving down highway 21 and, to their surprise and dismay, they saw Barefoot Bubba's and Gay's Fish Company had taken a beating, as Grandfather would say. Johnson Creek Restaurant had been flooded, as well.

As Grandfather and Grandmother drove toward the front gate of the island, they wondered what they would find. Big trees had been cut to clear the road for returning folks to the island. Grandmother even thought about the children who lived in the neighborhood. "I certainly hope that Rose, Claire, Paige, and Krew made it to safety," Grandmother mused.

Grandfather smiled a huge smile at the sight of the Fripp Island sign! It was a welcome reminder of home to folks as they returned.

As Grandfather and Grandmother drove down Tarpon Boulevard, they noticed some houses had a lot of damage, but some did not...

Grandfather turned into their street and could see that the houses were all intact. That was a welcome relief!

Before long they made it to their house. Grandfather asked Grandmother to check the first floor, while he checked the back of the house. Grandfather really wanted to check the tree where Big Daddy loved to sit and watch.

Sure enough, there was Big Daddy sitting on the tree branch with a big grin on his face as Grandfather approached. Big Daddy jumped from the branch to greet Grandfather. They agreed they would meet at the crabbing dock to catch up on all the things that happened on the island and check on their animal friends.

After Grandmother and Grandfather assessed the house, they went to bed to get some rest. Grandmother fell asleep and Grandfather returned to the crabbing dock, finding it in bad shape. Hurricane Matthew had given the dock a good pummeling.

When Grandfather arrived, Big Daddy and Rico started to catch
him up on all that had happened on the island while they were
gone. Big Daddy had organized all the animals on the island—it
was especially helpful that he was bilingual. He met with the deer,
squirrels, birds, turtles, and even the alligators (but he decided not
to get too close to the alligators, just in case).

Big Daddy patiently updated his animal friends each day. Because he could speak English, he listened to the news daily and could relay the information to the other animals. The president from the Fripp Association published a Daily Post, so Big Daddy started to do the same. Each day, the animals gathered to hear the news from Big Daddy with Rico by his side.

During the storm, the animals were scared and hid in the woods, remaining as low as possible to avoid the hurricane. They found holes in trees to be especially helpful for safe hideaways.

Some of the smaller animals hid behind strong buildings and remained in hiding for days. The turtles moved to higher ground and dug holes for safe hiding.

Big Daddy told Grandfather that one huge alligator got so confused, he ended up going to the tennis court near the Beach Club! Now that was a sight!

As Frippers began returning to the island, families joined together to support and help each other. As Big Daddy reported to Grandfather each day about his animal friends, Grandfather told him how the clean-up of the island was going.

Big Daddy was excited that the National Guard came to assess the island and its bridges.

It was amazing to see all the volunteers working and helping others. FEMA came to the island and stayed for several weeks.

"What's FEMA?" Big Daddy asked Grandfather.

"FEMA stands for *Federal Emergency Management Agency*," Grandfather explained. "They go to areas after a disaster has happened to help rebuild."

The next day, the president of the island called a meeting at the chapel to give thanks and praise the many volunteers on the island. She asked for several folks to share their blessings and thanks to the group. Big Daddy and Rico watched from behind a pew in the chapel.

The president did a wonderful job sharing information and even related Hurricane Matthew to the book of Matthew in the Bible. As folks sat there you could hear a pin drop! Everyone was so thankful and moved by the analogy of Matthew 7:24 and what had happened on the island.

Amazingly, Hurricane Matthew helped make the folks—people and animals—who lived on Fripp Island all come together! There were animal volunteers and human volunteers.

As they all prayed together and gave thanks to all, they knew for sure they were blessed!

"Therefore everyone who bears these words of Mine, and acts upon them, may be compared to a wise man, who built his house upon the rock." – Matthew 7:24

We are Fripp Strong!

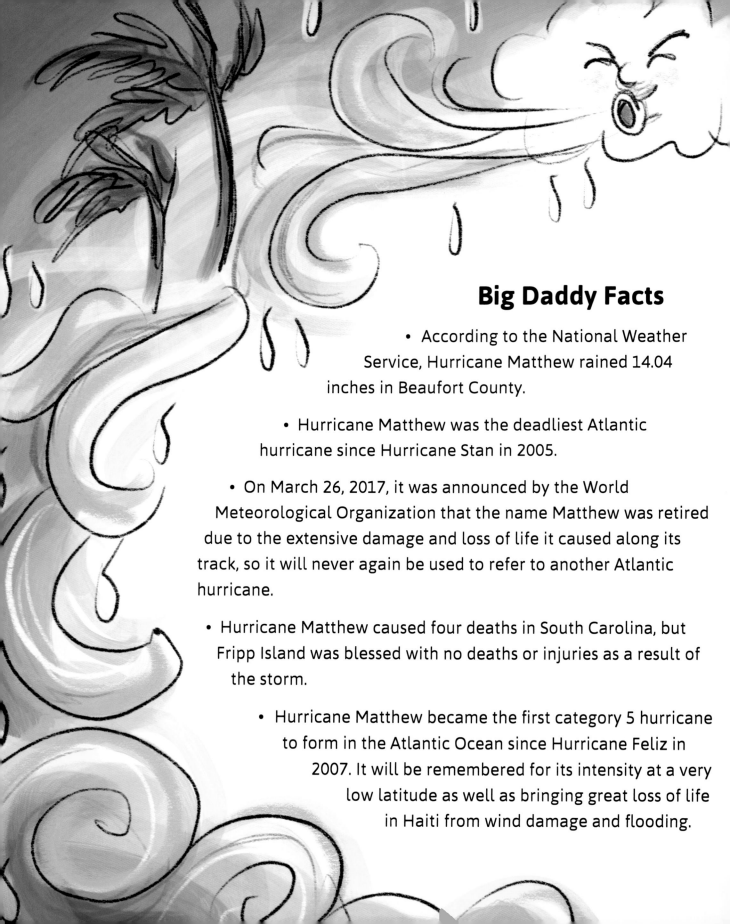

Big Daddy Facts

- According to the National Weather Service, Hurricane Matthew rained 14.04 inches in Beaufort County.

- Hurricane Matthew was the deadliest Atlantic hurricane since Hurricane Stan in 2005.

- On March 26, 2017, it was announced by the World Meteorological Organization that the name Matthew was retired due to the extensive damage and loss of life it caused along its track, so it will never again be used to refer to another Atlantic hurricane.

- Hurricane Matthew caused four deaths in South Carolina, but Fripp Island was blessed with no deaths or injuries as a result of the storm.

- Hurricane Matthew became the first category 5 hurricane to form in the Atlantic Ocean since Hurricane Feliz in 2007. It will be remembered for its intensity at a very low latitude as well as bringing great loss of life in Haiti from wind damage and flooding.

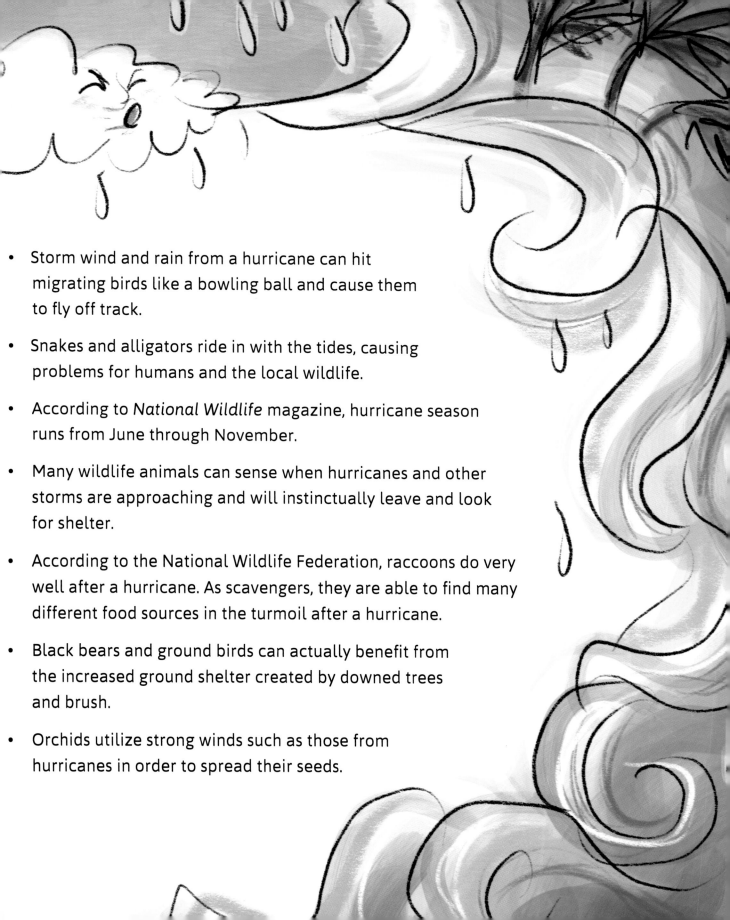

- Storm wind and rain from a hurricane can hit migrating birds like a bowling ball and cause them to fly off track.

- Snakes and alligators ride in with the tides, causing problems for humans and the local wildlife.

- According to *National Wildlife* magazine, hurricane season runs from June through November.

- Many wildlife animals can sense when hurricanes and other storms are approaching and will instinctually leave and look for shelter.

- According to the National Wildlife Federation, raccoons do very well after a hurricane. As scavengers, they are able to find many different food sources in the turmoil after a hurricane.

- Black bears and ground birds can actually benefit from the increased ground shelter created by downed trees and brush.

- Orchids utilize strong winds such as those from hurricanes in order to spread their seeds.

About the Author

Mary T. Jacobs is a retired middle school principal and college professor. She worked at Mercer University and was the coordinator of the Educational Leadership Department. She has two children and three awesome grandchildren. Mary currently resides on Fripp Island.

Mary has published many articles and is the author of *Inspiring Future Leaders through Coaching and Mentoring*.

Hurricane on Fripp Island: A Big Daddy Adventure is her fourth book in the Big Daddy series. Be sure to check out the other books—*Big Daddy's Secret on Fripp Island, Rico's Fripp Island Adventure,* and *Rico's Cabo Adventure.*